# Storybook

## Collection

This edition published by Parragon Books Ltd in 2014
Parragon Books Ltd
Chartist House
15–17 Trim Street
Bath BA1 1HA, UK
www.parragon.com

ISBN 978-1-4723-4915-6

Printed in China

# Storybook
## Collection

Bath • New York • Cologne • Melbourne • Delhi
Hong Kong • Shenzhen • Singapore • Amsterdam

# CONTENTS

Belle and the Castle Puppy     9

Cinderella and the Lost Mice     33

Ariel's Dolphin Adventure     57

Aurora and the Diamond Crown     81

Rapunzel and the Jewels of the Crown     107

Merida's Wild Ride     133

# BELLE AND THE
# CASTLE PUPPY

By Barbara Bazaldua

Illustrated by STUDIO IBOIX, Marco Colletti
and Elena Naggi

Belle was strolling through the castle garden one chilly spring day, when she heard a whimpering sound. A shivering puppy was huddled by the castle gates.

"Oh, you poor thing!" Belle cried. "Let's get you warmed up and fed!" She cuddled the puppy in her red cloak and hurried to the castle kitchen.

The enchanted objects laughed when he splashed in his bath. The dinner forks combed his fur while he gobbled a bowl of warm stew. Chip and his brothers and sisters giggled when the puppy drank water from them.

"He's so cute! I hope we can keep him!" Chip said.

But one enchanted object didn't join the fun.

The ottoman watched the puppy. He remembered when he had been a real dog. Suddenly, he wanted some attention, too. With a funny little "grrr," he thumped around the kitchen, trying to act like the puppy. But no one noticed.

Just then, the puppy bounded to the door, barking eagerly.

"Do you want to go out to play?" Belle asked, opening the door.

As Belle and the others followed the puppy outside, they didn't see the ottoman slink out and wander off alone. They laughed as Belle threw sticks for the puppy to fetch. Just then, the Beast walked up the path, clutching one of his precious rosebushes. "Someone has dug up my roses!" he exclaimed.

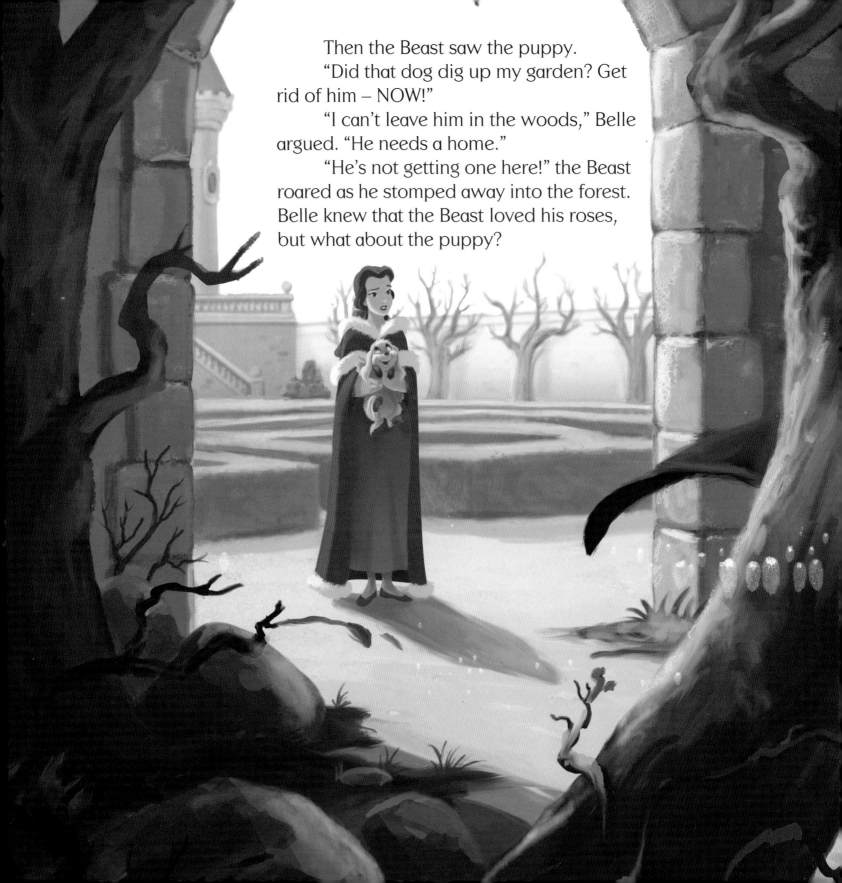

Then the Beast saw the puppy.

"Did that dog dig up my garden? Get rid of him – NOW!"

"I can't leave him in the woods," Belle argued. "He needs a home."

"He's not getting one here!" the Beast roared as he stomped away into the forest. Belle knew that the Beast loved his roses, but what about the puppy?

Just then, the ottoman ran past Belle and the others. His legs were muddy.

"Ottoman dug up the garden!" Belle exclaimed.

"But why?" Lumiere asked.

As Belle watched the ottoman racing after the Beast, she suddenly understood.

"Oh, poor Ottoman," Belle said. "He just wanted some attention, too!"

Suddenly, the
puppy raced after the
ottoman, barking playfully.
  Belle tried to call to them, but
they disappeared among the trees.
  "They'll get lost!" Belle exclaimed.
"I have to bring them back safely."
  "But it's getting dark," Mrs Potts protested.

19

Belle looked at the long shadows creeping through the forest and shivered. Clutching her red cloak tightly, she took a deep breath and started towards the trees.

"Wait!" Lumiere called. "I'll come and light your way."

"Thank you," Belle said as she held Lumiere up high. "I'm glad you're coming."

"Me, too. I think," Lumiere replied. But his flames flickered nervously.

"Puppy! Ottoman!" Belle called as she and Lumiere searched. Something rustled in the bushes. Yellow eyes gleamed at them.

"What is that?" Lumiere whispered.

"I hope it's just squirrels," Belle answered.

"It must be very big squirrels with very big eyes," Lumiere replied.

Belle picked up a large stick. Then she and Lumiere walked on, calling and calling.

Suddenly, they heard ferocious barking and snarling nearby. Belle ran towards the sound and stumbled into a clearing. The ottoman and puppy stood below an enormous tree. Snarling wolves circled them. But the puppy was growling and snapping back.

"He's protecting Ottoman!" Lumiere exclaimed.

"He's too small to stop those wolves for long," Belle answered. "He needs help!"

Quickly, Belle put Lumiere on the ground and lit the stick with his flames. Turning swiftly, Belle ran at the wolves, swinging the blazing stick at them like a flaming sword. "Get away! Get away!" she shouted. Snarling angrily, the wolves backed away from the fire. Belle raced between them towards the ottoman and puppy.

But just then Belle tripped on a root. The
torch flew from her hands. "Oh, no!" she gasped.
The torch hit the ground and rolled
just out of her reach. The growling wolves
crept towards her.

Barking fiercely, the puppy raced to the flaming stick. He snatched one end in his teeth and darted among the wolves. As the wolves backed away, the ottoman ran in front of Belle, yapping for her to follow.

"The puppy's clearing the way!" Lumiere shouted. "Follow Ottoman!"

29

Suddenly, the Beast crashed into the clearing. The wolves scattered yelping with fear.

The danger had passed. But the puppy's nose and ears were singed and sore.

"He and the ottoman tried to save me!" Belle said.

"They are brave little fellows," the Beast answered. Cradling the puppy in one arm and the ottoman in the other, he led Belle to the castle.

When the puppy was cared for, everyone settled by the fireside. Belle watched the Beast stroke the ottoman and feed the puppy biscuits. The gentle smile on his face made her happy.

"May the puppy stay until I can find him a home?" she asked.

The Beast cleared his throat. "His home is here – with us," he answered gruffly. Belle smiled, knowing the Beast loved both of his pets dearly.

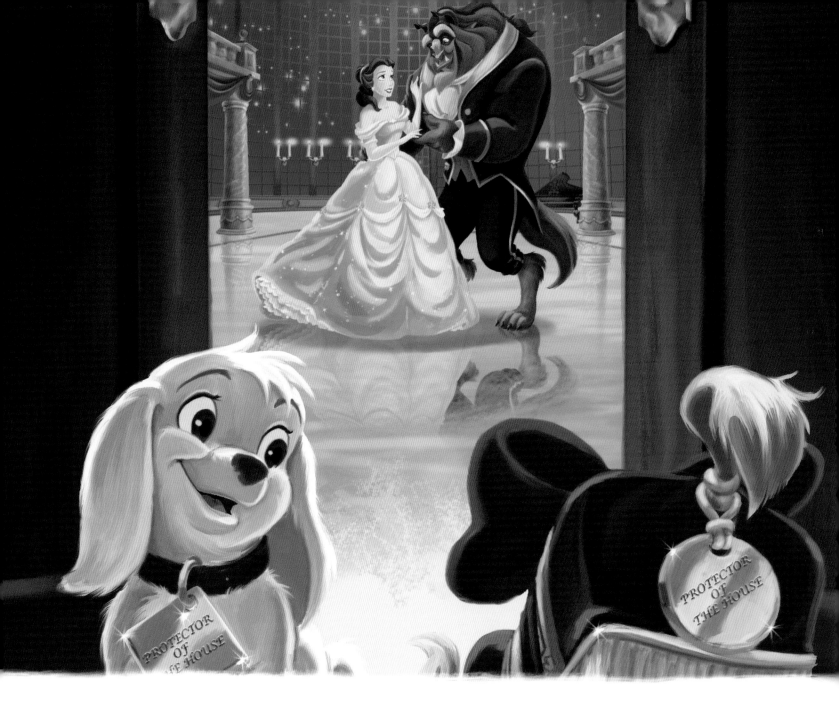

The next evening, as Belle and the Beast waltzed in the ballroom, the puppy and ottoman kept guard proudly at the door. Both the puppy and the ottoman wore shiny new badges. And on each badge were the words, "Protector of the House."

*The End*

# CINDERELLA AND THE LOST MICE

By E.C. Llopis

Illustrated by: IBOIX and Michael Inman

The stars twinkled in the clear night sky as the Prince twirled
Cinderella outside to dance.

"Are you cold, my dear?" the Prince asked his princess.

"Just a bit, but –"

Smiling, the Prince reached for a box he had hidden under
the bench. Inside was a beautiful winter coat.

"Oh, it's simply lovely!" Cinderella exclaimed. "Thank you!"

The next morning, Cinderella showed her coat to Suzy the mouse. "Isn't the Prince kind to me?" she said.

"Nice-a! Nice-a!" Suzy nodded and nuzzled the warm coat.

Cinderella didn't notice that Suzy had just come in from the cold. The tiny mouse was shivering even though the room was warm!

Just then, Gus and Jaq scampered up onto Cinderella's dressing table.
"Cinderelly! Cinderelly!" they chattered.

Cinderella didn't hear them as she rushed off to meet the Prince. She didn't
know that they were cold, too!

Soon, several more cold and shivering mice entered the room. They sat in front of the fire until their teeth stopped chattering. The poor mice had spent the night in the freezing attic! They hoped Cinderella would let them stay in her warm room. But there was a problem.

"Shoo, shoo!" The cruel housekeeper barged into the room and began chasing the mice! "You're making the whole castle dirty!" she shouted. "I should have the gardener haul you away!" She was the reason that the mice were cold – and scared! They stayed in the attic to hide from her!

The mice scrambled back to the chilly attic, not knowing where else to go.
"Cinderelly," Gus sighed. They needed her help!

Suddenly – *WHAM!* – the gardener slammed cages over the mice and scooped them up!

"Now take them outside!" shrieked the housekeeper.
"Take them far enough away that they never return!"

Of course, Cinderella had no idea what had happened as she and the Prince strolled around the castle grounds.

"Let's go to the stables!" Cinderella said suddenly. "We can say hello to the horses."

"And maybe take a ride?" the Prince asked hopefully.

"Lovely idea!" Cinderella replied.

Soon Cinderella and the Prince were riding through the countryside near the castle. They saw the gardener doing something in one of the fields.

"Hello!" shouted the Prince. "It's too cold to be working outside!"

But the gardener didn't seem to hear the Prince.

When the Prince and princess returned to the stables, the Prince asked, "Do you think the gardener was acting oddly?"

"Perhaps he was distracted," Cinderella replied thoughtfully. "It must be hard to do much gardening when the ground is frozen."

47

But the gardener was not distracted about gardening. He was worried about the mice! He knew that they would freeze in the fields.

"All right," he said to his helpers. "Now don't mention this to the housekeeper, but I want to bring these poor mice to the stables."

So they took the grateful mice to their new home and even fed them.

The mice nestled together in the barn, but as night approached, they just got colder. Finally, the horses allowed them to snuggle up in their manes to keep warm.

"Thassa nice-a," Gus said sleepily.

Meanwhile, Cinderella was beginning to worry. Where were her little friends?

"Jaq and Gus!" she thought suddenly. "They wanted to talk to me this morning, but I left in a rush to see the Prince. I wonder if they needed to tell me something."

Cinderella was searching the palace trying to
find her friends when she ran into the Prince.
"Why, hello!" the Prince said cheerfully.
"Are you looking for the same person I am?"
"Person?" asked Cinderella. "Why, no!
I'm looking for the mice!"

"Ah," said the Prince. "And I am looking for the housekeeper who apparently threw them out of the castle today. She said they were dirty!"

"Dirty! Oh, no!" Cinderella cried. "They're not dirty. And besides, they'll freeze outside!"

"Don't worry, my dear. The mice have found a new friend." The Prince then told Cinderella about the gardener and what he had done.

Together, Cinderella and the Prince went to the stables, where they found and thanked the gardener. Then Cinderella awakened the mice who were snuggled comfortably in the horses' manes.

"Cinderelly! Cinderelly!" the mice shouted happily.

A few nights later, there was a grand ball – with the gardener as the guest of honour. The cruel housekeeper now peeled potatoes in the kitchen. She would not be bothering the mice again. Meanwhile, the mice celebrated with a banquet of their own. And as for the horses, they got extra apples all around!

*The End*

# ARIEL'S DOLPHIN
# ADVENTURE

By Lyra Spenser
Illustrated by IBOIX and Andrea Cagol

"Oh, Eric! This is wonderful!" Ariel said excitedly, as she twirled around the ballroom with her prince. "I can dance with you and see the ocean!"

"Do you miss your sea friends?" he asked.

"Sometimes," Ariel replied a bit sadly. "But I love being with you."

Bright and early the next morning, Prince Eric found Ariel walking along the beach. He knew that she was hoping to see Flounder and Sebastian, as well as her other friends. Sadly, they were nowhere in sight.

Eric caught up with his princess and hugged her as they watched the white-capped waves crashing hard against the shoreline.

"It's rough out there today. If I were a fish, I think I might be too scared to come close to shore," Eric said gently. "Don't worry, Ariel. We'll figure out a way to bring together land and sea. You deserve the best of both worlds."

Later that day, Eric
and Ariel went for a walk.

"I was thinking about what you said
earlier," Ariel said. "I want to show you
something." She led him straight to a quiet,
beautiful little lagoon.

Eric grinned. "I almost kissed you for the first
time here."

"Eric, do you think my friends would
feel safer visiting me here?"

Eric rubbed his chin. "Hmmm. Maybe."

A few weeks later, Eric found Ariel walking along the beach again.

"Come with me," he said. "I have a surprise for you."

He took her straight to the lagoon. It now had a big wall to keep out dangerous sea creatures like sharks, but it also had a gate so that Ariel's friends could enter the lagoon. In fact, Flounder, Scuttle and Sebastian were there to greet her!

"Oh, Eric!" Ariel gasped. "I love it!"

Ariel was so
excited that she waded into the water.
Then she stopped, seeing something
else in the lagoon. "Look!" she exclaimed. As they watched, a baby dolphin leaped out
of the water! "He's just a baby. I wonder where his mother is."

Flounder swam across the lagoon, but the baby dolphin raced away.

"Poor little guy," Flounder said. "He seems scared of me."

"We should find his mother right away!" Ariel said, as she gently coaxed the baby to swim over to her.

"I bet she's on the other side of that wall. Don't worry, Ariel!" Flounder said. "We'll find her!"

But Sebastian and Flounder couldn't find the dolphin's mother. "Oh, Ariel! This is terrible," Sebastian said a few days later. "We have looked everywhere under the sea, but cannot find the baby's mother. King Triton will be so angry!"

Ariel was watching the little dolphin swim slowly around the lagoon. Heartbroken, she knew that the confused baby was looking for his mother.

Later that night, Ariel awoke to the sound of a loud clap of thunder. From the safety of the palace, she saw terrible, high waves crashing on to the shore.

"Ariel?" Eric asked. "Are you worried about that baby dolphin?"

"Oh, Eric, I am. He must be terrified," she shuddered in reply. "We need to go to him. And, Eric? I need to ask my father for help."

Eric felt terrible. He now understood that he had made a bad decision by closing in the lagoon. He followed Ariel into the stormy night, ready to help in any way he could.

When they arrived at the lagoon, Flounder was trying to calm the frightened baby dolphin.

"Go to the baby dolphin, Eric," Ariel said gently. "He feels safe with you."

Ariel looked into her prince's eyes, letting him know that she trusted him with her sea friends.

73

Ariel climbed carefully out onto the wall of the lagoon and called to all the sea creatures.

"Help me, please!" she cried out. "I am Ariel, princess of the seas. I need my father, King Triton. Please help!"

Below the surface, sea creatures raced to find King Triton.

Eric tried to keep the baby dolphin safe from the crashing waves. Holding him, Eric led him to the calmer waters near some rocks. Suddenly, there was a flash of light and the storm calmed. King Triton had arrived at the lagoon.

"What has happened here?" King Triton roared.

Eric looked down humbly. "It is entirely my fault, Sir," he explained. "I built this wall to make a nice place for Ariel to visit her friends. I was wrong."

The king of the seas glared at Eric. Then, with a hint of a smile, he added, "Well, you are human, after all."

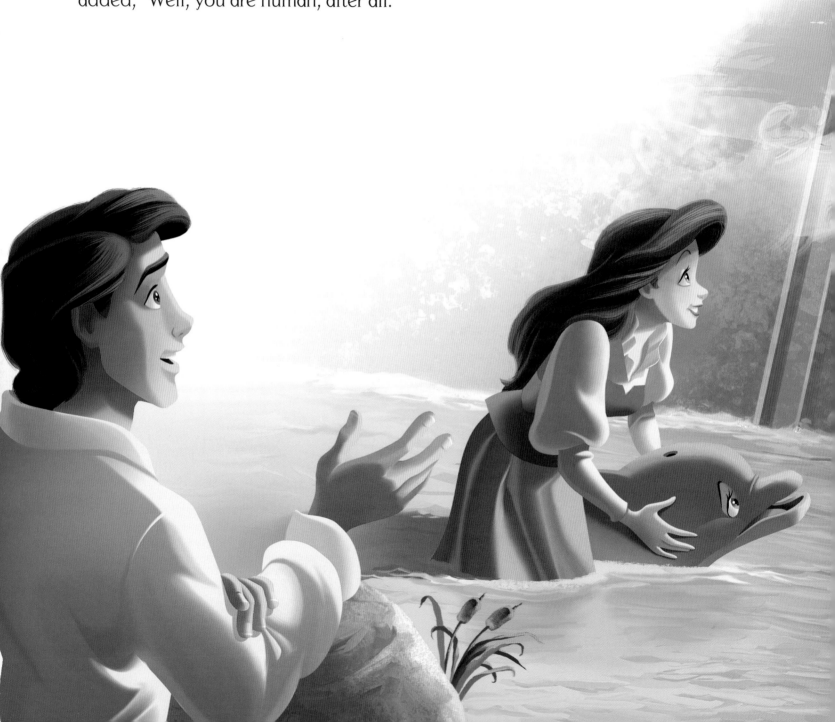

With a wave of his trident, King Triton called to all the dolphins and they quickly found the baby dolphin's mother! Frantically, she tried to get into the lagoon.

"Oh, dear!" Ariel exclaimed. "The gate won't open! She can't get in!"

Eric looked at King Triton. "Do you mind?"

"Not at all," the king replied. "Swim back, everyone!" He raised his trident and blasted down the wall.

There was no royal ball that night at the palace. Instead, Eric and Ariel returned to the lagoon and danced under the sparkling stars.

"I love this place," Ariel said to her husband. "Thank you."

Just then, the baby dolphin and his mother entered the lagoon, surfaced and playfully splashed the prince and princess.

"I think that means we are forgiven!" Ariel laughed.

*The End*

# AURORA AND THE DIAMOND CROWN

By Barbara Bazaldua
Illustrated by STUDIO IBOIX, Marco Colletti
and Elena Naggi

Aurora awoke one sunny morning in the most cheerful of moods. After all, it was her seventeenth birthday and she could not wait to see what wonderful surprises were in store.

Luckily, she did not have to wait too long. As soon as she was dressed, her mother, the Queen, came in. Aurora noticed her mother was wearing a crown Aurora had never seen before. Gleaming at its centre was a large, pink, heart-shaped diamond trimmed all around with tiny, sparkling diamonds.

"Mother!" she cried. "What a beautiful crown! Is it new?"

"Actually," replied the Queen, "it's quite old. And it's the reason that I've come to you so early on this very special day."

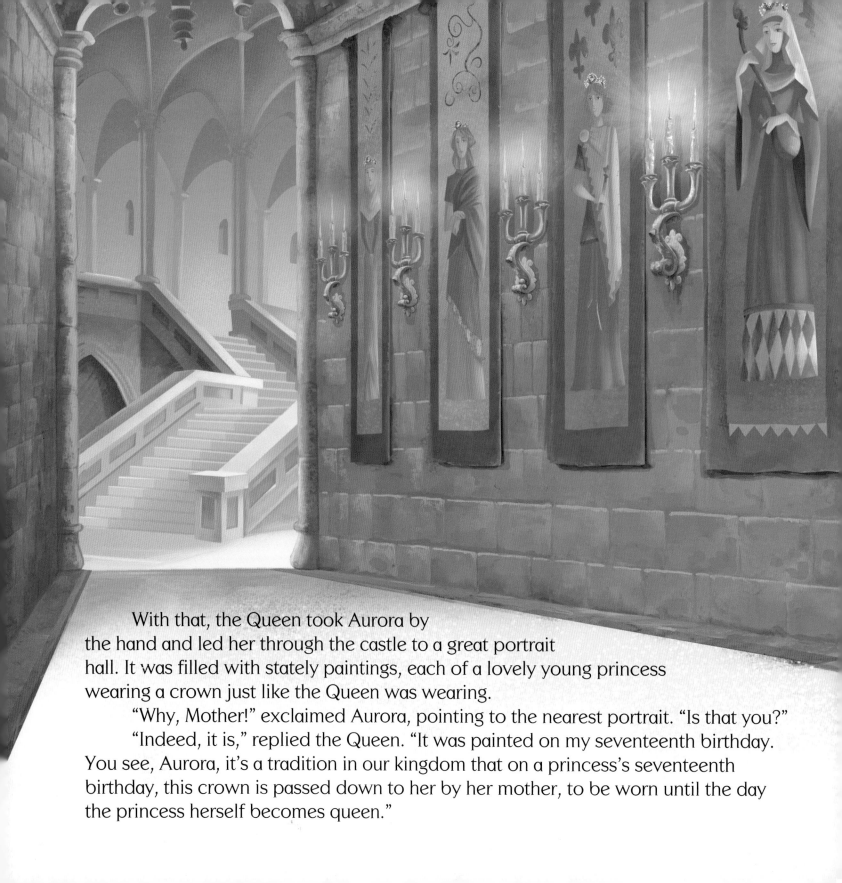

    With that, the Queen took Aurora by
the hand and led her through the castle to a great portrait
hall. It was filled with stately paintings, each of a lovely young princess
wearing a crown just like the Queen was wearing.

    "Why, Mother!" exclaimed Aurora, pointing to the nearest portrait. "Is that you?"

    "Indeed, it is," replied the Queen. "It was painted on my seventeenth birthday.
You see, Aurora, it's a tradition in our kingdom that on a princess's seventeenth
birthday, this crown is passed down to her by her mother, to be worn until the day
the princess herself becomes queen."

"Oh, Mother!" Aurora gasped. "Is that crown truly to be mine?"

"Well," her mother said with a smile, "I certainly hope so! But, according to tradition, you must first earn it."

"How?" asked Aurora.

"By answering three riddles," her mother explained.

Just then, the three fairies, Flora, Fauna and Merryweather, flew in.

"Happy birthday, Princess!" said Merryweather. "We're here to give you your clues!"

Then the Queen kissed Aurora. "Think hard, my dear. And good luck!"

With a wave of their magic wands, the fairies made themselves bigger and transported themselves and Aurora out onto the castle grounds. Then Flora stepped up and recited the first riddle:

"To the eyes, it's a treat; to the nose, a delight.
But beware! To the hand it can be quite a fright.
Though few think to taste it, its sweetness still shows.
To this first riddle, the answer's a…"

"Hmm…" said Aurora when Flora was done.
"Oh! I know!" said Merryweather.
"Of course you know," scolded Fauna. "It's Aurora who has to guess!"
"Do you know what the answer is, dearie?" asked Flora.

"Let's see," said Aurora. "'To the eye, it's a treat.' So it's pretty… 'To the nose, a delight.' So it smells good… 'To the hand… quite a fright.' So it must hurt… like a thorn… on a rose. That's it, isn't it?" And she hurried off to the rose garden, where she picked the biggest, most fragrant rose she could find.

"Very good!" exclaimed Fauna. "And now for the second one:

*Some plant it, some steal it, some blow it away.*
*Some do it several times in a day.*
*Some who are shy might blush getting this*
*On their hand or their cheek.*
*Can you guess? It's a...*"

"Well…" said Aurora, thinking. "If 'some plant it,' it might be another flower – a dandelion, perhaps? You can blow them away, too. Of course, we don't have any of those in our garden. But what can you get on your 'hand' or your 'cheek'…?" she wondered aloud as she gazed at her reflection in the garden pool.

"I know!" Aurora cried suddenly. "It's a kiss, isn't it?" And, as if to prove it, she planted a kiss on each of the fairies, causing them to blush.

"Honestly," said Flora, "you're figuring out the answers more quickly than any princess yet!"

"Now it's my turn!" exclaimed Merryweather. "Are you ready, Aurora?"

"I think so," she replied.

"Ahem." Merryweather cleared her throat.

> *"What only gets stronger the longer it lives?*
> *What pays you back tenfold the more that you give?*
> *Some say it's blind, some say it's true,*
> *Some just say simply, 'I… feel this… for you."*

Merryweather giggled. "Silly me! I almost said the answer!"

"Well, let's see," said Aurora. "It
might be a tree. That 'gets stronger the
longer it lives.' And I suppose you could
say that a tree is 'blind.' But so are bats…"

Aurora was still thinking when Prince Phillip
walked by, leading his horse, Samson. "Happy birthday, my
love!" he called with a big smile. And instantly, Aurora knew
what the answer to the riddle was.

Happily, Aurora hurried back to the castle and to her mother's room.

"I've solved the riddles!" she announced. She took the pink rose from her hair and handed it to her mother as she kissed her on the cheek.

"Very good!" declared the Queen. "And the answer to the third riddle?"

That's when the fairies brought in Prince Phillip.

"It's love," said Aurora, "of course!"

No sooner had Aurora said the word than the Queen took the crown from her head and proudly placed it on Aurora's.

And then, some say, the heart-shaped diamond shone even brighter than before!

That very afternoon,
Aurora had her portrait
painted just as all the clever
princesses who had come
before her had.

And that night there was a grand birthday ball held in the castle in Aurora's honour.

"Happy birthday, Aurora, my darling," her mother told her warmly. "And may you have many, many more!"

The End

# RAPUNZEL AND THE JEWELS OF THE CROWN

Rapunzel was excited! Freed from her tower and Mother Gothel, she and her friends were travelling back to the kingdom. Soon she would meet her true parents, the King and Queen.

"I can't believe I'm the lost princess," said Rapunzel. "I don't know how to be a princess."

Flynn smiled and said, "You'll be great as a princess. All you have to do is wear a huge, heavy crown...."

110

"Oh, my!" Rapunzel exclaimed.
"– though it's not a requirement,"
Flynn added quickly.

111

"Let me start over," Flynn said. "Do you remember that tiara from my satchel? Well, let me tell you a story about that.

"When I was a kid in the orphanage, I read a book about the princess and her tiara. The book said this tiara symbolized everything the princess should be.

"The tiara's white crystals stood for a strong, adventurous spirit; green represented gentleness and kindness; red stood for courage; and the round golden crown itself stood for leadership.

114

"For years, I thought of that tiara and then one day, I actually met a gal who could wear it. She certainly was adventurous....

"As she travelled towards her dream, she also showed kindness towards everyone, courage and definitely leadership. She just seemed to be able to turn every bad situation into something wonderful!"

"Flynn, are you talking about –?"
Rapunzel started.

"You!" Flynn exclaimed. "I'm talking about all those amazing things you did when you left your tower in search of those floating lights."

"But I did all those things when I had long, magical hair!" Rapunzel exclaimed. "Now I can hardly stand up straight. I feel off-balance. I have no idea how to help anyone without magic."

Suddenly, they heard a commotion behind them.

"Nobody move!" someone shouted. Several men were ready to attack! "Just hand over your horse!"

Flynn leaped into action, chasing the thieves. "Rapunzel!" he shouted. "Run away and don't look back!"

But Rapunzel did not run away. She ran right into the middle of the fray, trying to rescue Maximus.

Flynn leaped onto Maximus' back. But the horse accidentally bucked Flynn off as he fought against the thieves.

When it was over, Rapunzel scolded the bandits.
"It's all my fault," one man replied. "I need your
horse to take my son to the doctor."

"Oh, my! Where is he?" Rapunzel asked.

Within minutes, Rapunzel was tending to the boy's injuries. He smiled in relief as he was hoisted onto Maximus for a ride to the kingdom's doctor.

"How can you ever forgive us?"
the men asked.

Rapunzel thought of
the tiara – adventure,
kindness, courage and
leadership. Suddenly, she
realized she didn't need her magical hair.
"Come with me," she said.

128

At the kingdom, Rapunzel received her princess crown and she knew no one would ever be as supportive as her faithful new friends!

The End

# MERIDA'S WILD RIDE

It was a soggy, stormy afternoon. Merida sat in the stables reading from an old book of Highland tales. She and her horse Angus wanted to go for a ride. If only the weather would clear up.

"Look, right there," Merida said. "Magical horses. That one there is called a kelpie. It's a water horse."

Angus snorted, shaking his head. It was clear that he wanted nothing to do with magic, especially after their last encounter.

The raindrops slowed and the clouds scattered.

"Come, lad," Merida said to Angus. "The sun's breaking through. Let's go for a ride."

They galloped across the bridge and down the hill.

Just as they reached the woods, a flash of grey caught
Merida's eyes. "What was that?"

But Angus didn't want to follow – whatever it was. "Don't
be a ninny," Merida chided him. "I'm sure it's not a bear."

Merida guided Angus to a clearing. In it stood a magnificent grey horse. Its coat shimmered. Its mane was like fine silk.

Breathless with excitement, Merida whispered to Angus, "I know that horse is magical."

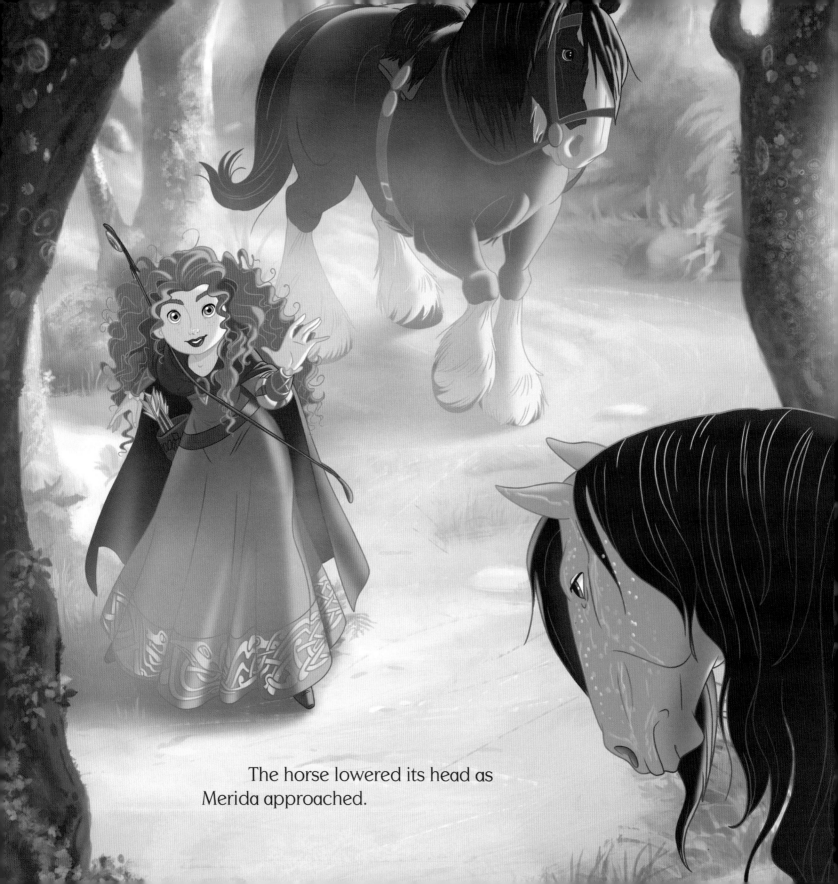

The horse lowered its head as
Merida approached.

Suddenly, Angus blocked Merida's path.
"Angus," she called, "Don't be jealous, lad! This horse
must be lost. We need to help him – make sure he's safe."

Merida talked to the grey horse, and it responded with a soft whinny.

Merida swung onto its back. She didn't have a bridle,
but she knew she could guide him with her hands wrapped in
his mane. The horse bolted but Merida wasn't frightened. She
had been around horses all of her life.

Merida tried to calm the horse. But he ran on. They were heading towards a large loch – a deep, dangerous lake.

Why did it seem as if her hands were stuck to the horse's mane? Were they entangled in his hair?

The horse brushed against a tree and trapped rainwater fell down on her. Effortlessly, one of her hands came free.

Just ahead, a bridle hung from a tree. Merida stretched to reach it as they passed, but it was just beyond her fingertips. "Angus, help! The bridle!" she called.

Merida could only hope that her friend had heard her cry. There was a cliff ahead, between them and the loch. *He'll stop before we get to it,* Merida thought. *Won't he?*

Merida tugged and pulled on the horse's mane.
Nothing worked. She even tried to slide off his side.
But she couldn't move.

Merida looked up at the sound of a whinny. Angus galloped up next to them – and he was carrying a bridle!

He tossed it. Merida caught it and slipped it over the horse's head. With the reins in her hand, she guided the horse to a path that led away from the cliff's edge.

As they reached the shore of the loch, the horse
finally slowed to a stop. Merida was no longer stuck.
She jumped off.

The stallion stood quietly. Merida looked in his eyes for an answer to what had caused the wild ride. Something sparked her memory and she removed the bridle. His head moved softly as if he were nodding, before he galloped down the misty shoreline.

Merida frowned as she watched him. Was he really racing into the water, or was it the fog playing tricks on her eyes?

Back at the stable, Merida looked at the book she had been reading. She found the legend of the kelpie. "Once a bridle is put on a kelpie, the water horse will do your bidding," she read.

She looked up at Angus. Was it possible? Had she been riding a kelpie?

# The End